Honey the and Kentucky Proud

MW00890044

Hannah Edelen Shelby Sawyer

Honey was a horse that lived
in central Kentucky

on a farm with her friends
where she felt so lucky!

She spent her time reading and
writing to grow as a horse

and often received letters from those
that wanted to learn more.

and decided to open her services
to expand her reach.

One day, Honey received
her first letter

from two little girls who
were on quite the endeavor.

Honey chuckled to herself and
then she started to write.

She wanted to tell Maddie and Tay
about the Kentucky might...

...about how farmers across the
Commonwealth work day and night

to meet the needs of the
many bluegrass families.

So Honey, with the permission
of the Edelen family,
loaded up the girls for a
field trip of glee!

Food to the Table

Bluegrass Animals

KY Bees at the Apiary

Farmer's Market

At the first stop, Maddie & Tay learned
about how food gets to the table.
It starts with a farmer...

then it's off to be labeled, sorted,
processed, and more! Following this
stage, it's off to your store.

"Wow!" Maddie said. "Yipee," Taylor exclaimed.
Our farmers work hard to make
sure we can eat.

Honey knew the journey was not over yet,
there was more to learn and
animals to pet!

At stop two, the girls visited some of
the state's best farmland
known as the bluegrass region
where agriculture is grand!

Maddie and Tay learned about
the state's main crops...

like corn, soybeans, hay--
the list doesn't stop!

While learning about crops, the girls heard
a few chickens. They clucked, bwoked,
and were on a mission!

The cows were in a huddle eating some
hay and the horses were neighing
trying to play!

At stop three, the girls learned about bees
in a place called the apiary,
where honey is their expertise.

Dipping their fingers on a comb,
Maddie and Tay felt right at home.

They learned more about the art of beekeeping, colonies, and pollination.

When it comes to helping make Kentucky's food, bees rise to the occasion.

The last stop was a trip to
the Farmer's Market.

It was the farmer's and community's
local red carpet...

...with baskets of veggies and meat on trays,
boxes of goodies, and smiles on display.

With the help of Honey, the girls grabbed
some treats to make their visit
and learning complete!

After a long day of learning,
Honey came back to the question
to see if the girls had learn
anything from her lesson.

Maddie and Taylor, with their
sugar rush from sweets,
shouted with joy and jumped
to their feet!

"Kentucky Proud is all about the bluegrass people,
their hard work, and the goods they
bring to the table.

It's about farmers, traditions, and connection
from crops to animals-- a wide selection.

It's the feeling of being proud when you've
worked very hard and want
to sing out loud!"

Honey said, "Yes! That is Kentucky Proud!
where the people are thankful,
and the spirit is loud!"

From the farm to the table,
Kentucky shows how they're able
to take a seed and meet the
need of our beautiful
bluegrass community!

A Note to Caregivers and Educators

Thank you for taking an interest in teaching the next generation about Kentucky Proud- Kentucky's official marketing program that promotes Kentucky's farmers, farm families, and farm impact products. Farmers play an essential role in ensuring that Kentuckians near and far have food on their table. By helping young people understand where their food comes from, we can have a meaningful impact on educating informed connections between food they consume, and the agricultural processes involved in producing it.

Follow-Up Activities:

Discover new information!
- Read about Kentucky Proud
- Learn about Agriculture
- Visit KY Proud on Social Media

Connect with farmers and people!
- Visit a Kentucky Proud Farm
- Tell a friend about KY Proud

Take Action in your world!
- Write a farmer a thank-you card
- Create your own Kentucky Proud Recipe
- Plant your own crop, flower, etc.
- Draw your favorite food and write a sentence about where it came from!

Where does food come from?

Food comes from many places.

Plants are grown in fields, gardens,
orchards, and farms.

Animals are taken care of by farmers
and other animal specialists.

Most groceries are made from food on farms, but
there are different kinds of farms.

Chickens and turkeys are raised on farms!

Eggs come from chickens - white eggs, brown
eggs, even colored eggs!

Beef cattle - gives us hamburgers, steaks, and roasts!

Dairy cattles gives us milk that helps us make yogurt,
butter, and more!

Orchards grow fruits like apples, peaches,
cherries, and oranges!

Bacon, sausage, ham and pork chops… come from pigs!

Corn, wheat, and rye are grains that are grown in fields.
Grains are ground into breads and cereals!

Lakes and oceans provide us with fish and seafood!

Potatoes, beets, radishes, and carrots grow under the
ground in vegetable gardens!

Other vegetables grow above ground like green beans,
tomatoes, squash, cucumbers, and peas grow on
vines and plants!

This book is in honor of my grandparents
- Bud and Bessie Yates- who were proud farmers.

I grew up learning many lessons from them on the farm like
the value of hard work, the beauty of patience, and the impact of
being a servant. They believed that if you had faith the size of a
mustard seed, you could move mountains. They deeply loved and
contributed to the community of Washington County where they
participated in church gatherings, attended local events, and had a
hand in making sorghum at the annual Sorghum Festival. Not only were
they farmers, they were the mother and father of nine children,
leaders in the community, and living examples of
kindness and goodness.

While they sowed many seeds in their lifetime to feed their
community and family, they sowed one of the most important seeds to
all those they encountered- LOVE.

Meet the Author & Illustrator!

Hannah Edelen, Author

Hannah Edelen is Miss Kentucky 2022 and the Official Spokesperson for Kentucky Proud, Kentucky's agricultural marketing brand. Hannah is a native Kentuckian, clogger, reader, teacher, horse enthusiast, and aunt to Madelynn and Taylor Edelen. Inspired by her childhood of growing up on a farm and her role as Miss Kentucky, Hannah chose Honey, Madelynn, and Tayler to share the story of Kentucky Proud. Hannah often shares how the ability to read gave her power. She has used her power to champion the cause for literacy and has taken her state program across the nation as "Read Ready America". Read Ready America is a literacy initiative with the goal of equipping individuals with the power to change the world through reading. Hannah wants youth to be able to find their power through reading!

Shelby Sawyer, Illustrator

Illustrator, Shelby Sawyer, currently works as a Graphic Designer in central Kentucky. She loves her family, friends, nature, art, and everything about Kentucky. Growing up in rural Kentucky, she grew up understanding the importance and value of her bluegrass community and all the hardworking people making it such a wonderful place to live. Shelby hopes to portray her love and pride for Kentucky by giving life to Honey and her adventures with Kentucky Proud!

What is Kentucky Proud?

For generations, Kentucky farmers have bred the best racehorses, grown grains and corn to make the world's greatest bourbon, and kept families fed here at home and across the country. Farming isn't easy, but it is essential. Here at Kentucky Proud, we're all about the continued promotion of agricultural products sourced from Kentucky's farms.

Introduced by the Kentucky Department of Agriculture in 2002, the Kentucky Proud brand (which was originally launched as Kentucky Fresh) was created as a central platform to raise awareness of the Commonwealth's ever-expanding agricultural efforts and to promote Kentucky's farmers, farm families, and farm impact products. In 2008, Kentucky Proud officially became the Commonwealth of Kentucky's agricultural marketing brand by legislative action, and the rest, as they say, is history!

The Kentucky Proud program is funded through the generosity of the Kentucky Agricultural Development Fund. Directed by the Kentucky Agricultural Development Board and administered by the Kentucky Office of Agricultural Policy, the fund is a product of the 1998 Master Tobacco Settlement between cigarette manufacturers and 46 states, including Kentucky.

There's a good chance you've seen the Kentucky Proud logo on products while shopping at your local grocery store or on a billboard off the side of a road. You may have caught a commercial on TV or heard a friend mention Kentucky Proud after visiting a farmers' market. But have you ever wondered what Kentucky Proud really does?

At heart, we're a local agricultural marketing program...

Friends, if variety is the spice of life, it's safe to say that Kentucky Proud is super spicy. But seriously, locally grown Kentucky Proud peppers are great. Kentucky strawberry preserves are our jam. Fresh cut flowers? We're digging those as well. Heritage breed lamb shanks on the menu at an awesome restaurant? Ewe better believe it. Suffice to say, if it's grown or raised on a Kentucky farm, we're passionate about it, and we want to make finding all those local products as easy as pie. And yes, we also love Kentucky Proud pies.

Our roots are in Kentucky soil...

Kentucky Proud promotes locally grown food, farmers' markets, farm stands, agritourism sites, and many other products and destinations here in the Commonwealth. Kentucky Proud products are raised, grown, or processed in Kentucky by Kentuckians. You can serve Kentucky Proud foods or purchase Kentucky Proud products with the confidence that they came from your friends and neighbors just down the road - not from thousands of miles away.

Dig up more on how we help farmers - and consumers...
To say we simply offer farm marketing services doesn't come close to covering enough ground. From exciting promotions and strategic media campaigns to grants for members and event sponsorships, Kentucky Proud is all about connecting consumers who are eager to find the very best from Kentucky farms with local farm businesses and quality products.

KENTUCKY
HORSE COUNCIL

The Kentucky Hose Council (the KHC) is a charity that helps horses all over the state of Kentucky. It doesn't matter if it's a trail horse, show horse, racehorse or anything in between - we love them all! The KHC does things like:

- Help horse owners who have been through floods and tornadoes
- Make sure hungry horses have food
- Train people to help horses that are in danger
- Offer all sorts of fun events for horse lovers
- Provide horse health info and a super calendar of events

We're best known for our license plate, which shows a foal lying in the grass. Learn how to become a youth member and how YOU can help horses in Kentucky by visiting kentuckyhorse.org

Honey the Horse

and Kentucky Proud

Hannah Edelen   Shelby Sawyer

Kentucky Proud

Honeycomb

Made in the USA
Thornton, CO
09/21/23 15:58:34